minedition

North American edition published 2014 by Michael Neugebauer Publishing Ltd. Hong Kong

Illustrations copyright © 2014 Keiko Kaichi
Original title: Der Wolf und die sieben Geislein
English text translation by Anthea Bell
Rights arranged with "minedition" Rights and Licensing AG, Zurich, Switzerland.

Michael Neugebauer Publishing Ltd., Unit 23, 7F, Kowloon Bay Industrial Centre,
15 Wang Hoi Road, Kowloon Bay, Hong Kong.
e-mail: info@minedition.com
This book was printed in April 2014 at L.Rex Printing Co Ltd 3/F., Blue Box Factory Building,
25 Hing Wo Street, Tin Wan, Aberdeen, Hong Kong, China
Typesetting in Adobe Caslon Pro.
Library of Congress Cataloging-in-Publication Data available upon request.

ISBN 978-988-8240-77-7

10 9 8 7 6 5 4 3 2 1
First impression

For more information please visit our website: www.minedition.com

Brothers Grimm

The Wolf
& the
Seven Kids

Keiko **Kaichi**

translated by

Anthea Bell

minedition

Once upon a time there was an old goat who had seven
little kids and loved them as all mothers love their children.
One day she wanted to go into the forest to get some food.
So she called all the kids to her and said, "Dear children,
I have to go into the forest. Be on your guard against the wolf;
if he comes in he will eat you all – skin, hair, everything.
The wolf often disguises himself, but you will always know
him by his gruff voice and black feet."

The kids replied, "Dear mother, we will take good care of ourselves; don't worry!"
So mother goat bleated and went on her way feeling happy.

Not much later someone knocked at the door and called, "Open the door, dear children, your mother is here and has brought something back for all of you." But the little kids knew that it was the wolf by his gruff voice.

"We will not open the door," they cried. "You are not our mother! She has a soft, kind voice and your voice is gruff. You are the wolf!"

So the wolf went away to the shop and bought himself a great lump of chalk, ate it and made his voice soft. Back he came and knocked at the door of the house, calling, "Open the door, dear children, your mother is here and has brought something back for all of you." But the wolf put his black paws against the window and the children saw them and cried, "We will not open the door. Our mother does not have black feet like you; you are the wolf!"

Then the wolf ran to a baker and said, "I have hurt my feet, rub some dough over them for me." And when the baker had rubbed dough over his feet, he ran to the miller and said, "Throw some white flour over my feet for me." The miller thought to himself, "The wolf wants to trick someone" and refused, but the wolf said, "If you won't do it, I will eat you." And the miller was afraid, so he made the wolf's paws white for him. What a weak man!

So now the wolf went to the door for the third time, knocked at it and said, "Open the door for me, children, your dear mother has come home and has brought all of you something back from the forest."

The little kids cried, "First show
us your paws so we may know you
are our mother." Then he put his
paws in through the window, and
when the kids saw that they were
white, they believed all he said
and opened the door. Then who
should come in but the wolf!
The kids immediately ran to hide.

One hid under the table,
the second in the bed,
the third in the oven,
the fourth in the pantry,
the fifth in the cupboard,
the sixth in the washing-bowl,
and the seventh in the
grandfather clock.

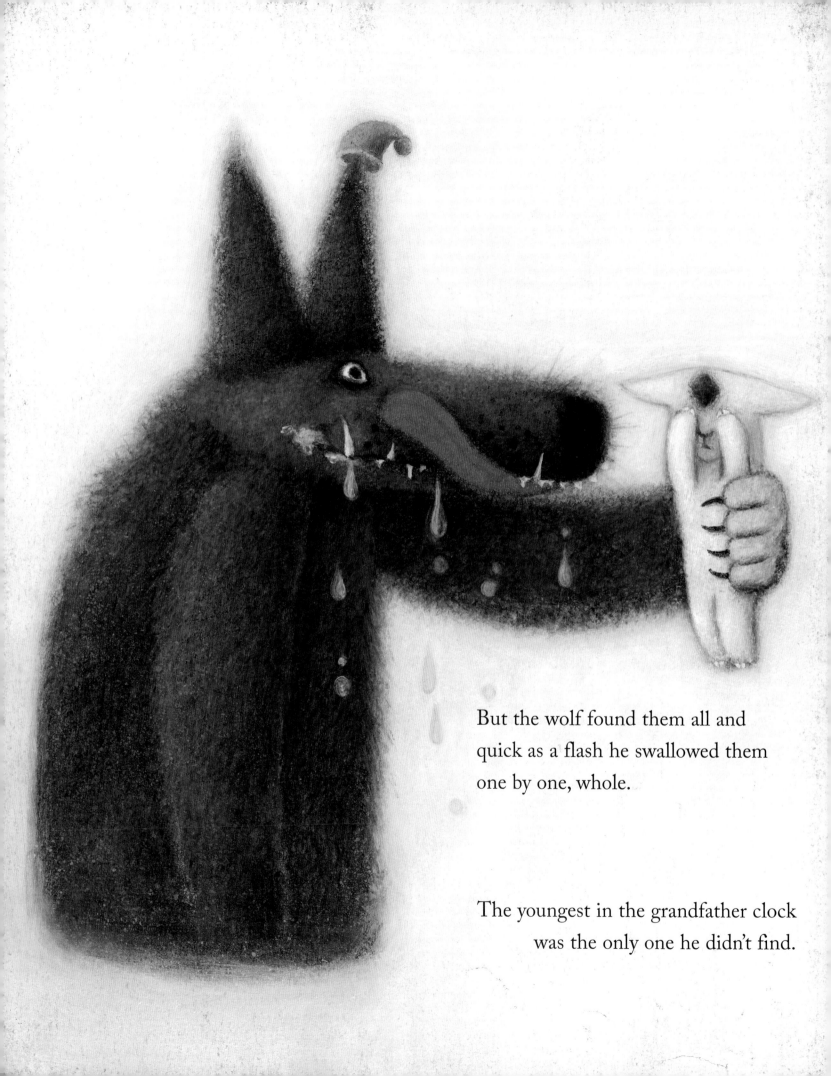

But the wolf found them all and
quick as a flash he swallowed them
one by one, whole.

The youngest in the grandfather clock
was the only one he didn't find.

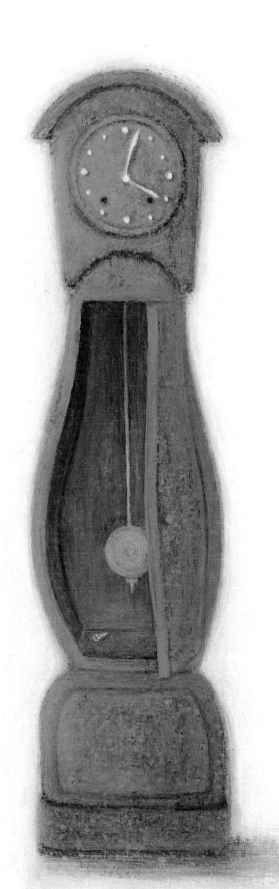

When the wolf was full up he left, laid down under a tree in the green meadow outside and went to sleep. Soon after the mother goat came back from the forest.

Ah! What a sight greeted her! The door stood wide open. The tables, chairs and benches were knocked over, the washing-bowl was broken into pieces, and the quilts and pillows were pulled off the bed. She looked for her children but they were nowhere to be found. She called them one after another by name but no one answered. At last, when she came to the youngest, a soft voice called, "Dear mother, I am in the grandfather clock." She took the kid out, and he told her that the wolf had come and had eaten all the others. Then how she wept over her poor children.

At last, sadly, she went outside, and the youngest kid ran with her. When they came to the meadow they saw the wolf by the tree, snoring so loudly that the branches shook. She looked at him closely and could see that something was moving and struggling in his huge belly. "Ah, heavens," she said, "could it be that my poor children whom he has swallowed for his supper can still be alive?"

Then the kid had to run home to fetch scissors and a needle and thread, and the mother goat cut open the monster's stomach. Hardly had she made one cut than a little kid thrust his head out, and when she cut further out sprang all six, one after another, all still alive, and they were not hurt at all, for in his greediness the monster had swallowed them down whole.

How happy they all were!

Then they hugged their dear mother. She said, "Now go and look for some big stones and we will fill the wicked beast's stomach with them while he is still asleep." Then the seven kids dragged the stones over as fast as they could and put as many into his stomach as they could get in and the mother quickly sewed him up again so that he was not aware of anything and didn't stir.

When the wolf at length woke he stood up, and as the stones in his stomach made him very thirsty, he wanted to get to the well to drink. But when he began to move about the stones in his stomach knocked against each other and rattled. Then he cried:

> "*What rumbles and tumbles*
> *Against my poor bones?*
> *I thought it was six kids,*
> *But it feels like big stones.*"

And when he got to the well and stooped over
the water and was just about to drink,
the heavy stones made him fall in.
There was nobody to help him,
and he was never seen again.

When the seven kids saw that, they came running to the spot and cried aloud:
"The wolf is dead! The wolf is dead!"
and danced joyfully around the well with their mother.

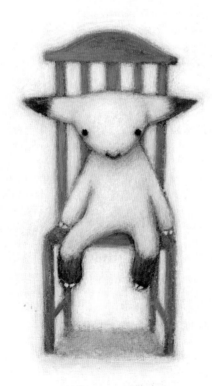